W9-DBO-166

Book 6

THE JUPITER TWINS

VACATION ON VENUS

BY JEFF DINARDO

ILLUSTRATED BY DAVE CLEGG

RED CHAIR ·PRESS·

Funny Bone Books

and Funny Bone Readers are produced and published by

Red Chair Press LLC   PO Box 333   South Egremont, MA 01258-0333

www.redchairpress.com

About the Author

Jeff Dinardo's books are filled with humor and silliness that captures a child's imagination. When not writing, Jeff runs a successful design firm specializing in textbooks for use in classrooms from K-8.

About the Artist

Dave Clegg lives and works on a small horse farm in north Georgia with his wife Lyn and their two children. All of Dave's work is done digitally on his computer. When he is not drawing, he can be found creating songs with his guitar or making robot sculptures!

Publisher's Cataloging-In-Publication Data

Names: Dinardo, Jeffrey. l Clegg, Dave, illustrator. l Dinardo, Jeffrey.
    Jupiter twins ; bk. 6.

Title: Vacation on Venus / by Jeff Dinardo ; illustrated by Dave Clegg.

Other Titles: Funny bone books. First chapters.

Description: South Egremont, MA : Red Chair Press, [2019] l Interest age
    level: 005-007. l Summary: "When it looks like their vacation is going
    to be really boring, space racers save the day until the race comes to
    a roadblock! Can the Twins pull out all the stops to rescue the race?"--
    Provided by publisher.

Identifiers:ISBN 9781634407519 (library hardcover) l ISBN 9781634407557
    (paperback) l ISBN 9781634407595 (ebook)

Subjects: LCSH: Twins--Juvenile fiction. l Neptune (Planet)--Juvenile
    fiction. l Outer space--Exploration--Juvenile fiction. l Racing--
    Juvenile fiction. l Vacations--Juvenile fiction. l CYAC: Twins--
    Fiction. l Pluto (Planet)--Fiction. l Outer space--Exploration--
    Fiction. l Racing--Fiction. l Vacations--Fiction.

Classification:LCC PZ7.D6115 Juv 2019 (print) l LCC PZ7.D6115 (ebook) l
    DDC [E]--dc23 l LCCN: 2018955671

Printed in United States of America

0519 1P CGF19

CONTENTS

MEET THE CHARACTERS

TRUDY

TINA

MS. BICKLEBLORB

MAX

🚀 OLD BETSY

Trudy and Tina were sitting in the backseat of the old tractor as it slowly chugged along the hills of Venus.

"This is the most boring vacation ever," said Trudy. "Good thing I packed some books."

"Be nice," said her twin sister Tina.
"We came to help Ms. Bickleblorb and Max."
It was true. Their teacher and her
scientist husband had invited the girls to
Venus to help them study the planet.

Max patted the steering wheel as they slowly drove along.

"I call her Betsy," he said. "She has been through a lot, but still has some good miles left in her."

They stopped in a barren stretch of land and hopped out. The girls helped Max and Ms. Bickleblorb unpack the scientific instruments.

As the adults worked, Trudy and
Tina walked around. Trudy saw an
outcropping of rocks with some berries
growing under it.

"Well, there is some life on Venus!"
she said. Trudy grabbed a fistful of the
berries and put them in her backpack.

"I hear something," said Tina as she walked over the next ridge.

Trudy walked up beside her.

10

Out in the distance they saw something heading toward them. It sounded like engines revving.

"What is that?" said Trudy.

"I don't know, but it's headed this way," added Tina.

Suddenly a large group of strange-looking cars came barreling down the hill. They seemed to be having a race.

Trudy and Tina could see all kinds of aliens driving past them.

"Space racers!" said Trudy. "I've heard about them. They race all over the galaxy. Let's follow them."

The twins ran after the racers.

"Stay out of trouble!" yelled Ms. Bickleblorb.

3 A CREATURE

When the twins got to the crest of the next hill, they saw all the racers stopped. They were at the entrance to a large tunnel. The drivers were all arguing and yelling.

The twins could see that a giant, blue blubbery creature with two snail-like eyes on its head had blocked the tunnel. It seemed to be stuck.

"I think we should stay away," said Tina.

"Nonsense," said Trudy as she ran to join the racers. "Let's see what is going on!"

"Come on, get out of the way," yelled one racer.

"We have to go through the tunnel!" yelled another, waving her tentacles.

The giant creature just looked bored and closed its eyes. It didn't seem to mind being stuck where it was.

4 A Good Idea

Some of the racers even tried to
push the big, blue, blubbery beast from
the entrance. But it wouldn't budge.
Trudy and Tina ran right up to the front.

"Maybe we can help," she shouted.

"How?" said Tina.

"Maybe the answer is in a book,"
said Trudy.

She reached into her backpack and pulled out the books she had packed. "Ah, here it is," she said. *"Aliens of the Universe."*

The racers watched over her shoulder as Trudy flipped through the pages.

She kept looking up at the creature,
then back down at the book.

"Not this one," she said on one page.

"Hmmm, not this one either," she said
as she flipped to another page.

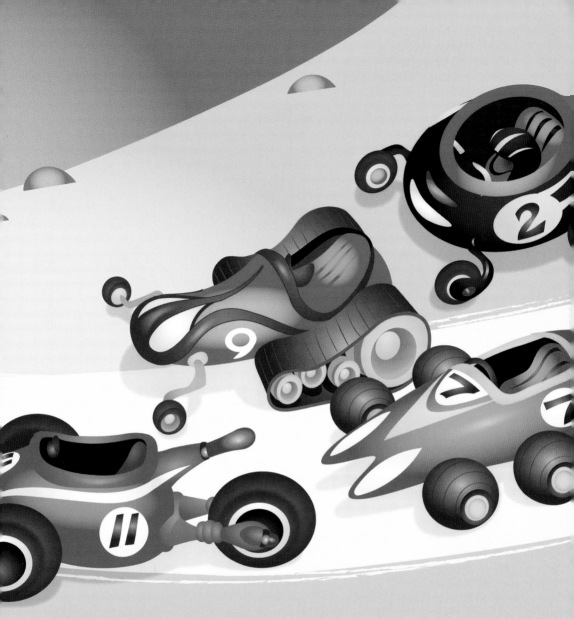

Tina nudged her sister. "Even if we
find the creature in the book, how will
that help us?" she asked.

"One step at a time," said Trudy as
she kept flipping through the pages.

"Ah ha!" she said as she finally
pointed to a picture in the book. It
showed a giant, blue blubber creature
with two snail-like eyes on its head.

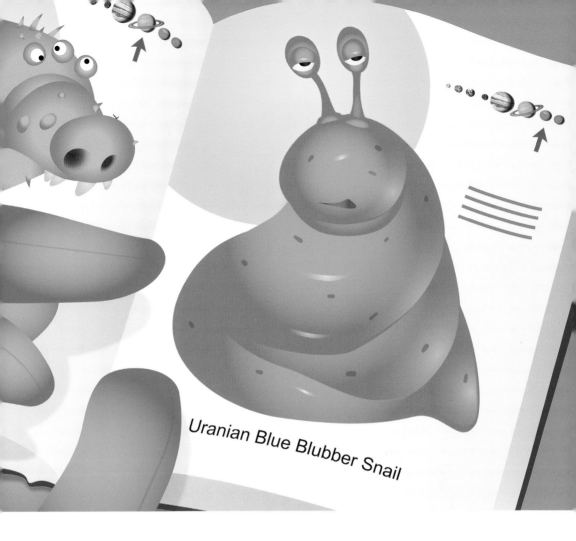

Uranian Blue Blubber Snail

"It's the *Uranian Blue Blubber Snail!*" said Trudy.

"What's it doing all the way out here on Venus?" said Tina.

Trudy read the text under the photo. "I'm not sure, but it says the Uranian Blue Blubber Snail's favorite foods are berries."

WILL IT WORK?

Trudy put down her book. "I have an idea how we can get the snail out of the tunnel!" she said.

She called all the racers and Tina together and told them her plan.

"When I say 'pull,' then you PULL HARD!" yelled Trudy.

All the racers were positioned at the entrance of the tunnel surrounding the Uranian Blue Blubber Snail.

Tina was standing with her hands behind her back just out of reach of the creature.

Trudy signaled her sister. "Now!"
she said.

Tina pulled her hands out and opened
them. She held the red berries that Trudy
had found.

The Uranian Blue Blubber Snail
suddenly sniffed the air. It saw the berries
in Tina's outstretched hands and smiled.
It stretched its blubbery neck out but it
could not reach.

The beast tried to pull itself out of the
tunnel to get the berries, but it was really
stuck.

"PULL!" yelled Trudy, and all the
racers grabbed a handful of the snail's
blubber and pulled with all their might.

"Is this going to work?" Tina asked
nervously.

Trudy grabbed the snail and pulled too.

The snail started to slip out.

"Here we go!" said Trudy.

PLOP

Out plopped the blue snail. And it instantly slurped up the berries from Tina's hands. It smiled contently and then quietly slid out of sight.

"Gross," said Tina, who looked at the blue snail goo all over her hands.

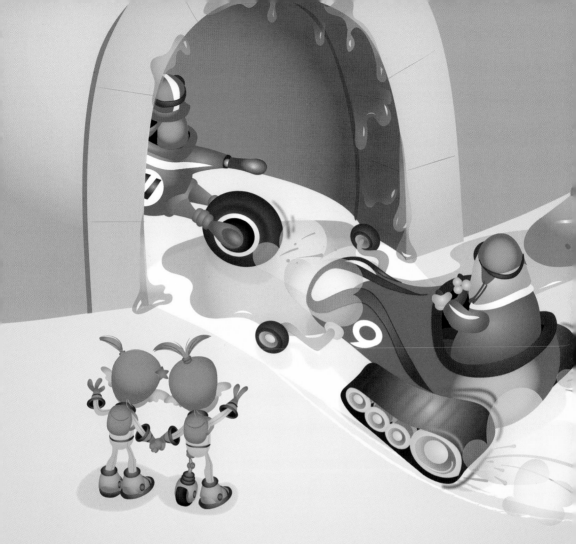

"It worked!" shouted all the racers. They all hugged Trudy and Tina before quickly jumping into their race cars. Then they sped off through the tunnel to continue the race.

The sisters were sad to see them go. "Now what?" said Tina.

Just then Ms. Bickleblorb and Max
came speeding over the ridge and stopped
in front of them. Old Betsy the tractor
looked like she had been turned into a
racing car.

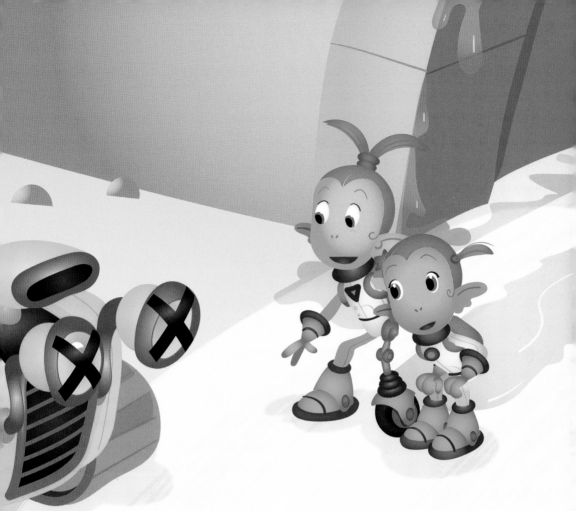

"We saw what you girls did to help," said Ms. Bickleblorb. "So Max did some work on Old Betsy."

"Hop in if you want to catch up to them!" said Max.

The girls hopped onto the tractor and buckled up.

Max put it into gear and they sped
off faster than they had ever gone before,
racing through the tunnel.

"*Jumping Jupiter!*" said Trudy.
"This is the best vacation ever!"

Her sister agreed.